BATTLE WITH SCHIZOPHRENIA;

SUHASINI'S VICTORY

GAYATRI JAITLY

First Published in June 2022

ISBN: 978-93-93809-08-7

BLUEROSE PUBLISHERS
www.bluerosepublishers.com
info@bluerosepublishers.com
+91 8882 898 898

Cover Design:
Geetika

Typographic Design:
Namrata Saini

Distributed by: BlueRose, Amazon, Flipkart

Dedication

I would like to dedicate this book to my grandparents - Late Mr. O. P Mohla and Savitri Mohla, Late Mr. M. S. Jaitly, and Shakuntala Devi. And all the people who have hope in their hearts.

Foreword

It is my pleasure to write the foreword for this book. As a Psychiatrist, I have seen many people battle with Schizophrenia and how it changes the life course of individuals. The description of the journey of Suhasini is honest and enlightening and captures the difficulties faced by people with the disorder.

But the book is not about the struggle, it is about hope, the ability to deal and cope with life. It is about resilience and a never give up attitude. There is much to share and much to learn from the experiences.

I take this opportunity to congratulate the author for writing this book. It will be extremely beneficial for many, will motivate people, and provide hope. And it will help the family and society understand the journey of the individual with this condition.

I wish Ms. Gayatri the best and hope she continues to inspire people in future.

Dr. Sonali Bali

Consultant Psychiatrist

Delhi

Acknowledgment

I would like to express my gratitude to wonderful people who have stood by me, and encouraged me to dream.

Firstly, I would thank Almighty for giving me life and leading a beautiful journey.

Secondly, all my family members (both paternal and maternal) especially my uncle and aunt Mr. Deepak Mohla, Mrs. Neeta Mohla, my principal sir, Dr. V. K Barthwal who always encouraged me to give my best; my friends Shomila, Pushpa, Rupam who stood by me like a rock; and my school colleagues who have always supported me.

Thirdly, my publishers, the amazing team at Bluerose who believed that this story should be shared with the world.

Most importantly, I would like to thank Dr. Sonali Bali for writing the foreword. She has captured the essence of the story in the foreword.

I truly believe that I am blessed to be surrounded by such genuine people. I thank all the people who have touched my life in some way or the other.

Preface

Battle with schizophrenia; Suhasini's victory is not just a story about a girl with mental illness but determination, the strength of character, and belief in oneself. In our society people with mental illness are looked down upon. If a person is diabetic, has **BP**, or even has a stroke, nothing abnormal is seen because it is a physical illness.

But if a person has a mental illness, he/she is considered less capable. Just visiting a psychiatrist is a no- no thing.

We need to change this scenario. Accepting people with mental illness will see a big change in society. Imagine you are sitting in a rose garden but you are constantly stressed and worried.

One is not able to enjoy the beauty of nature if one is mentally ill.

As Milton rightly said, "The mind is its place and, in itself can make a heaven of hell or a hell of heaven." So, it's the mind which rules the matter.

I sincerely hope that this story helps to bring happiness and joy to someone's life.

Author Bio

Hi! I am Gayatri Jaitly, a 46-year-old, alumni of Delhi Public School Mathura Road, New Delhi. I did English honors from Delhi University and later B.Ed. I am an educationist with over 20 years of experience, presently working with DAV Public School, Jasola Vihar, New Delhi.

I would like to mention here that I am the right person to write about schizophrenia because I, myself, have gone through it. It will be an eye-opener for people either suffering from it or for the near and dear ones who are looking after them. The names in the book have been changed to some extent to protect their identities.

It requires a certain amount of patience and compassion to deal with people suffering from schizophrenia. It is high time we understand different mental illnesses and not term everyone as "pagal" or mad. Schizophrenia is curable. With the right intervention, one can lead a normal life. This book should open a discussion about mental health so that as a society we become more receptive. I hope this book makes difference in someone's life.

Synopsis

This is the story of Suhasini, a girl who saw her father recover from a major accident. Due to the accident, her father lost the power of writing and his speech. Suhasini was six months old then. Her father was a Chartered Accountant.

She saw her uncle who had mania attacks and another uncle who was a drug addict. Due to this, there was constant bickering in the house, as it was a joint family. Life was a constant struggle. Her mother, Manjiri was a teacher in a reputed school. Suhasini was the only ray of hope for her parents as she would bring joy to their lives with her deeds and actions. Life was difficult, but due to her mother's spirits, it was not such a bad situation. She always said, "Count your blessings."

Suhasini's teenage years were not easy as she could not speak about family affairs with anyone. As a result, she remained in her shell for a long time. Until Sneha entered her life. She took care of her. Suhasini felt comfortable and secure in her company. She could connect with her.

One day in 11th, Sneha too left her. Her circumstances at home became worse after Suhasini's grandmother passed away. The circumstances were so bad that she had to take her board exams from her maternal grandfather's house. Unhappy with the result she tried to commit suicide. The guilt of not being able to embrace death was far more burdening than death itself. Finally, she got admission to Delhi University and was constantly worried about finances.

Suhasini after her third year went on to get a job in an advertising agency. Just as she was about to get the first pay cheque her uncle got hospitalised. After 3 days of struggle, he died. And left behind a difficult court battle to be fought. Now the entire family's responsibility came onto Suhasini's shoulder. Only her grandfather, mother, and father are left in this world. Manjiri had taken retirement due to her husband's and her ill health. With all these responsibilities Suhasini realized that an ad agency was not her cup of tea. She decided to do NTT and get a job as a teacher.

Once she got a job as a teacher, her grandfather passed away. Her aunt (Chachi) had already filed a legal petition against them. After rounds of negotiations between her mother and aunt, things are set straight. The house is set for sale and Suhasini's parents take another house elsewhere. Now, Suhasini has the time to focus on her career. She decides to do B.Ed. Meanwhile, as they move to the new house, in a month her father passes away. Suhasini goes into depression but recovers with the right intervention.

Now is the time for her to settle down. She gets married to Vikram. It is an arranged marriage. The marriage lasts for 2 years. They get divorced with mutual consent.

After her divorce, Suhasini decides to concentrate on her career. She gets a job in a reputed school. After one year, she is made permanent. But she gets an attack of schizophrenia. She feels cut-off from the rest of the world. She feels everyone can read her thoughts. Suhasini feels she is being controlled. All the years of stress accumulated gave rise to this. Suhasini's doctor tried to convince her but in vain. She remained in this situation for almost a year. Her medication continued. But her thought process did not change. It was difficult for her. Manjiri was determined to make Suhasini alright. But as they say, tough situations do not last, tough people do. At last, one fine day after many months Suhasini was speaking something relevant. The doctor was happy to see her progress. It was her childlike spirit and never say die attitude which kept her going even when the road was rough. She knew she had to fight and survive. Suhasini knew life isn't easy for everyone. She had to stand up for herself and conquer all difficulties. Suhasini exemplifies hope and courage. She exudes positivity.

Family tree

(Paternal grandparents) Pitaji and Jhaijee- (children) Ram, Gittu, Pappi. Ram married to Manjiri. (Suhasini's parents) Pappi got married. Gittu remained unmarried.

(Maternal grandparents) Papaji and Biji- (children) Pankaj, Mannat, Manjiri, Madhurima, Adarsh. Adarsh married to Anita (Suhasini's Mama, Mami)

Contents

Chapter 1

The accident

On 3rd August 1975, it was raining heavily. The roads were blocked, it was pouring since morning. Biji (Suhasini's maternal grandmother) had lost the house keys. She came running to the hospital where Manjiri (Suhasini's mother) was admitted. Right at

12:45 in the afternoon Suhasini came breathing into this world. Manjiri looked at her and said to herself "Doesn't look like me". She was waiting for her husband. Her husband had gone to Tehran.

When Jhaijee (Suhasini's paternal grandmother) was given the news, she distributed sweets in the gali. After that, she made panjiri and came to the hospital. After staying for a few days, Manjiri wanted to go back home as it was her birthday. They took Suhasini home on 12th August. But the packing led to a strain on Manjiri. This was the only year when Manjiri did not have an asthma attack, otherwise every rainy season she had an asthma attack. She promised herself that she will never be strict with her daughter. She will develop a good rapport.

Ram (Suhasini's father) meanwhile sent a beautiful card which said 'fairies made eyes of the baby, they chose rose to make lips and so forth'. Later years it touched Suhasini's heart when she saw this card as a teenager. Ram wanted Manjiri and baby to join him but had to wait at least six months. He was working as an auditor in a leading company.

Manjiri took Suhasini to Tehran in a plane. When she landed somebody was there to receive them. She inquired about Ram and was told just to go with them. On reaching home she was told that Ram met with a major accident due to which he lost his power of writing and speech. He was still in the hospital. The world came crashing down on Manjiri.

Manjiri was told about the best neurosurgeon in AIIMS. Still, Ram was under observation. They had to see how he would react to situations? How his memory was working? It was a challenging time for Manjiri. She wrote a letter to Jhaijee. Things were grim. It was a brain injury. After staying there for a few days Manjiri returned to India.

Chapter 2

At home

At home in Phool Mandi things were really bad. Pappi Chacha had a mania attack and Gittu Chacha was under the influence of drugs. Jhaijee was very affectionate. She wanted her nieces to stay with her after her brother passed away. Jhaijee loved the girls from the bottom of her heart. She was very fond of all her nieces. Everyone who met Jhaijee became her fan. She was a loving, courageous and compassionate lady. It was her large heartedness that could accommodate every single soul in that tiny house. The relatives, who stayed with them after partition, upon seeing the deteriorating condition of the family abandoned them. They were left to their destinies.

Ram used to use disconnected words and his language was meaningless. Manjiri and Pitaji (Ram's father) were the only earning members in the family. Suhasini was left with Jhaijee.

Manjiri started teaching Suhasini and Ram. It was difficult for a woman who was pampered and wanted her man to lead her. She spent sleepless nights looking after Suhasini and Ram. Another blow for her happened when, Biji passed away. She was completely broken. Once in Delhi Ram was taken to AIIMS for further investigations and treatment. Pitaji and Papaji(maternal grandfather) would go to AIIMS to see the doctor.

With great difficulty Manjiri was carrying on her job. Suhasini was growing up too. She demanded attention and was very playful. Meanwhile their house in Kalinga Vihar was given on rent. Ram wanted to move out of Phool Mandi as Suhasini was growing up. They moved to Kalinga Vihar and also found a playschool close by.

Everyday a maid used to come to pick up Suhasini for school. Meanwhile, Ram was on medication. One day he had epileptic fits. When Manjiri came back Suhasini told her. She was just five years old then. Next day he was taken to AIIMS and doctor said "If you had delayed the medicine by one day, it could have resulted in serious consequences". Manjiri hugged Suhasini and told her about the incident later.

Chapter 3

Childhood memories

Suhasini always wanted to have a big doll and a doll house. She wanted to have doll house with furniture and utensils. Suhasini was always fond of collecting such items. Whenever she would see these things Suhasini would insist on buying them.

She was also fond of wearing glass bangles. When she couldn't even speak Suhasini went down the lane to ask for matching bangles by showing her frock. But Suhasini never insisted that her mother buy chocolates and sweets like any other child.

In Kalinga Vihar there was a gurudwara where they would recite "wahe guru, wahe guru" every morning and evening. As a curious child of 3 years Suhasini asked her mother – "Where is this sound coming from?"

But Manjiri was so busy in the home affairs that she couldn't answer her query. Once Manjiri was buying vegetables, Suhasini quietly slipped and crossed the road to go to Gurudwara. After an hour, when there was no sound in the house Manjiri and Ram began to wonder where Suhasini had gone. They were shocked to find her missing. It was turning dark. They went here and there and thought of complaining to the police. After sometime they saw Suhasini coming out of gurudwara. They thanked their stars.

Suhasini was happy at playschool. She got a certificate in Art competition. Ram and Manjiri proudly went to see her painting. Her name was announced in the assembly when Suhasini got admission in reputed school due to her artistic skills.

Ram's only mission meanwhile was to get the tenants to leave the house in Kalinga Vihar. He couldn't speak but was determined to get the house vacant.

Meanwhile Suhasini's Mamaji (maternal uncle), Adarsh got married. Suhasini felt her Anita Mami had just come for her. She felt Mami was hers. That's what a five year old thinks.

Suhasini was an extrovert. She used to participate in dance and poem recitation. She was very demanding as a child. Manjiri could only control Suhasini's demands by saying "If you cross your limits, I will tell Mamaji.". Because Suhasini was afraid of him. She was not scared of Manjiri and Ram. Children are born fearless. We instil fear in them. Manjiri had to instil fear in her so that Suhasini did not harm herself.

Suhasini and Manjiri had gone to one of the emporiums in Baba Kharak Singh Marg. Manjiri was not listening to Suhasini. They went to the first floor but Suhasini was interested what was happening on the ground floor. Suhasini accidentally pushed Manjiri's bag and the glass came crashing down. The whole emporium became silent. Suhasini was thrilled. Manjiri turned around and caught hold of Suhasini. But Suhasini walked like a princess. Manjiri went apologizing to the people for the damage done.

Suhasini loved her teachers of class prep and in class I, her first cousin was born (Adarsh's son). Suhasini was thrilled. She thought that we go to hospitals to get babies and this thought remained with her till she was 17.

Once in school as a five-year-old Suhasini had participated in ballet —The selfish giant. Suhasini was playing the role of child who brings about change in the giant. She was very friendly with the senior class boy who was playing the giant's role. But when the make-up was done, he looked so horrifying that Suhasini shrieked and ran away. She hid in some corner. People went hunting for her. Suhasini was nowhere to be found. Time was passing by - the ballet had to start. Suddenly, one of Aya didi found her and convinced her to come out. They coaxed her to come with them and see Bhaiya. Finally the make-up was removed to show the real face and Suhasini believed it was the same Bhaiya.

Even though Manjiri used to teach in the same school, Ram or her grandfather would sign her report card. Suhasini used to wonder in school "Why does everyone inquire about my father?" "He is fine but why do people talk about him?" It was a sensitive issue with her. Meanwhile, Suhasini kept participating in Art competitions and winning prizes. By fifth standard, she was made Director of Art and Craft of primary wing.

This was the stage to figure out who was your best friend and who would be your worst enemy? Who would give you notes and who would complain against you? Suhasini was standing at this juncture. Suhasini could easily make friends. She was an honest child who was transparent in her dealings. But there was so much competition regarding picking up friends and academics. She was talented and wanted to learn new things every day. There were some children who were jealous of her which is expected. But there were some who really liked her for who she was. Suhasini was an outgoing child brimming with enthusiasm. She wanted to learn music, dance and sketching. Her parents wanted her to excel in academics too, as she was a bright child.

Chapter4

Joint family

Ram and Suhasini shared one common interest of movies. They loved watching comedy movies. They bonded over it.

Meanwhile in 1984 Suhasini's Chacha got married and in came her Chachi. One did not know this was the beginning of different battles to be fought. Once she reached sixth standard, Suhasini started commuting independently in the bus. Now she was in the middle school. Suhasini was a bright student who participated in co-curricular activities especially music. She got a badge for securing more than 75%.

Ram meanwhile got a job in the government sector but was regularly getting transferred. The problem was his speech and many people misunderstood him. He was a simple man and did not understand office politics.

Suhasini and her family were staying at Kalinga Vihar and her Chacha and Chachi also moved in. In the meantime, Jhaijee, Pitaji and Gittu Chacha also shifted there. They were a typical middle-class family.

1986-87 was the golden period for Suhasini's family. Her cousin was born. Her Chacha – Chachi had a daughter. Pitaji and Jhaijee were becoming old and Gittu Chacha's ways were becoming difficult.

Ram and Pitaji disliked him because of his behaviour and always gave him warnings. But Jhaijee and Chacha supported him.

In 1988, Jhaijee had a cataract operation. Suddenly one day, Chachi left the house, leaving the child behind. As a child Suhasini was worried what had happened and missed her Chachi very much.

But from there, the fall of all the family members started. Her Chachi meanwhile filed a divorce petition. There was always tension in the house. Gittu Chacha and Chacha got along very well because they supported each other.

Pitaji used to beat Gittu and Ram used to run to see the condition and support Pitaji. There were abuses, beatings, throwing of things and all sorts of violence in the house. Suhasini could not study in that atmosphere. Her studies suffered the most. Whenever she sat to study abuses were hurled at each other. Beatings took place. Sometime the police were also called.

In 1990, Jhaijee died. They had to prepare themselves for more ugly things. Suhasini knew she had to do well in her studies but was unable to find a solution to her home affairs. They had difficulty in talking to neighbours because of the obvious problems. Still, she kept her head high. Suhasini still wanted to make friends in neighbourhood.

Chapter 5

Adolescence

Once in 8th standard, Ram introduced her to world of Ghazals and Urdu poetry. This made a huge impact on Suhasini. She found solace in ghazals. Suhasini could appreciate both English and Indian music. She could listen and learn ragas too. Music and dance programs kept the three of them together. Life was changing for Suhasini.

As a teenager, Suhasini found her best friend had deserted her. She became close to someone else. So, Suhasini too decided to find another friend till next year, she found Sneha.

Ram had already resigned from his government job. He could not cope up with family atmosphere and office politics. His recovery was left in between due to unstable home affairs. When anybody, her Masi or Mamaji, came from abroad, they went to meet them in Papaji's house. Suhasini got along well with all her cousins. She loved looking after them. The atmosphere in Kalinga Vihar was not presentable. For Suhasini there were no family vacations, they only went to Papaji's house. Papaji would talk, listen and get worried. He was concerned about Suhasini's future. Ram wouldn't leave his parents and things would not change.

As a teenager, Suhasini could not invite any of her friends to her place. She went to stay with them. Once Suhasini surprised Sneha by showing up at her place. Sneha was absent but Suhasini still went with her mother to Shivalik. They had a beautiful time. Sandy aunty was very warm and caring. These times were like balm on those harrowing times. These homestays came with a set of instructions- you will stay at one place; you will not go out anywhere or put yourself into trouble. As a teenager there were lists of dos and don'ts. Suhasini never cheated on her friends. She remained loyal to them. Their secrets were kept close to the chest. School was the place when she could be herself. Her home affairs were changing from bad to worse.

Wherever Suhasini went, Manjiri went with her. Manjiri gave her a diary to pen her thoughts. Manjiri told her "I will never read your diary, if you like to share then you can". As a teenager, Suhasini had her difference of opinion with Manjiri. But Manjiri said "I will never scold you. But if you hide something that means you are doing something wrong." So, her friends used to wonder how Suhasini could share everything with her mother. Manjiri was very gentle and always gave a patient hearing. Due to this, her relationship with Ram was also neglected.

The divorce petition with Chachi was going on. The drug abuse with beatings was on. Manjiri's physical health was deteriorating. Ram was almost losing his mental balance.

Suhasini chose commerce subject in 11th and moved to a different section. Her close friends chose other subjects. Suhasini moved to Papaji's house to take her board exams, as Chacha had a mania attack. Gittu Chacha left the house. Moving to her Nanaji's house meant changing tuitions and uprooting oneself. When her classmates were revising the course, she was looking for tuitions in the month of November near Papaji's house. With great difficulty they found one for Maths and Accounts.

After Suhasini returned from Papaji's house, Pappi Chacha took up her responsibility. He got her college books and made sure everything was available for studies. Suhasini was allowed to use his landline. Chacha took care of Suhasini for 3 years. He was very affectionate and missed his daughter who was very young. He loved children and used to pamper Suhasini. At first it was her Adarsh Mamaji who initiated her to wear lenses. But it was her Chacha who made this dream come true.

Ram meanwhile had gone into a shell. He developed a wall around him so that no one could reach him. Suhasini tried to pacify him many times but it was futile. After 12th board result was out, Suhasini was utterly disappointed. She didn't know who to blame. Suhasini started hating everything. She tried to commit suicide by slashing her wrists. Suhasini thought it was the end of the world. It was Pitaji's and Chacha's inspiring words that made her rise from the ashes. They had a firm belief that things could be turned around. Suhasini had the capability to rise again.

Suhasini thought as a teenager that destiny decides career, but realised in college that you make your own destiny. Suhasini started thinking 'What could be done to bail out her parents?'

Suhasini wanted to work but her Chacha said "Finish your education first." The moment she finished her education (took her third-year exams), she applied for a job. Suhasini got into advertising firm as a client servicing executive. They wanted to launch a new company for exhibitions, so they hired her. Suhasini was thrilled. Finally, she was going to be independent. But life has its bittersweet moments. The day she was to receive the pay cheque Chacha had fallen sick. He had to be hospitalised immediately. He struggled for 3 days and then died. Nobody was with Suhasini in the hospital. She was just 22 when she got the dead body home.

When the dead body was lying in the room, Pitaji said "Chal mera puttar khada hoja." He had turned into a stone, because Chacha was a devoted son. He took lot of precautions during Pitaji's cataract operation. He took good care of him. Suhasini realised that now was the time to stand together and sort out the difficulties. She had to take care of Pitaji, Ram and Manjiri. Somebody had to be strong so that no one takes advantage of their position. She had the urge to look for long term solutions. Suhasini had faith that things could be better. She thought carefully. She had a strong desire to make everything alright for the family. Suhasini had deepest regard for Pitaji and her parents.

Chapter 6

After Chacha's death

Pitaji couldn't even get up from the bed, after Chacha's death. It was Suhasini's duty to make him walk and stand on his feet. Once she was back from the office, it was her duty to make him walk. She would share his routine. But slowly Pitaji started smoking again. Suhasini knew he was broken. He was putting a brave front because he was the head of the family.

Slowly, Suhasini realised that she had too many responsibilities and couldn't continue working in an advertising firm. After six months, she opted for teaching. Advertising was not her cup of tea. Manjiri and Papaji wanted this. In all these tough times Kavita aunty (next door neighbour) always supported Suhasini. Kavita aunty always gave her a patient hearing. She was caring, loving and was genuinely concerned about Suhasini's welfare. She was a pillar of strength.

Suhasini started collecting information as to how to enter the teaching profession. Nursery teacher's training required 2 years, but she couldn't make a commitment for 2 years. Sometimes Pitaji, Manjiri or Ram had to be hospitalised. For Suhasini, it was a difficult situation. Soon she went to an institute which was conducting the program for one year. This was not recognised program. The principal there convinced her that two-year training was compressed into 1 year and they would equip her within that time frame. It suited her as it was near her place.

The training was tough and interesting. Experienced teachers shared their knowledge. It was very delightful. After completing the course, she applied for a job. She was selected but was taken on ad-hoc basis. This continued for 2 years.

Meanwhile Pitaji passed away. Everything fell on her. Within five months Papaji also passed away. This was a major blow for her. Suddenly she felt protective hands of her grandparents (paternal as well as maternal) were no more. Suhasini had to secure her parents' future. Chachi had already filed claim for share in the house and PF of Chacha. Chacha had nominated Suhasini. Now the negotiations had to start between Chachi and Manjiri, Ram. Ram and Manjiri were already in a fragile position. Their health was always an issue. The negotiations continued. After that it was decided that they will get half share in the house and Suhasini gave the PF amount to Chachi. Manjiri, Ram and Suhasini had remained honest in their dealings. Suhasini got this trait from her parents. Even though, Chachi was not there- still they regarded her as a family member.

Chapter 7

Professional course

It was time to move on. Suhasini was looking for an institute which was running a B.Ed. course. She wanted to do this through distance learning program but couldn't get through entrance test. It was decided to take this course from a nearby state. This had to be regular program, so she had to give up her job. Finally, she got admission in a college. She was thrilled and went to Sai baba mandir to offer her gratitude. At last God fulfilled her dream. She had to change three buses to commute to the college. Her journey started 5o'clock in the morning. But this was her priority.

Now was the time to shift to her new residence. Ram had become extremely weak. Something was eating him up. But just to bring joy in the family Suhasini got a mobile phone. While studying she had to inspect how the house was coming along.

Finally on 13th April 2003 they shifted to Mahanadi Nagar. It was Ram who decided the date. But in a month Ram died of a cardiac arrest. Suhasini went into depression. She remained continuously sad for days. With great difficulty Manjiri went to Suhasini's college. She met Priya her friend. Priya stood with Suhasini like a rock. Priya always encouraged her. She got help books for her. Priya was determined that Suhasini had to complete her B.Ed. Then she took a firm decision - COME WHAT MAY.

Priya went to the university office to sort out the exam details. And with her belief Suhasini was able to take her exams and come out with flying colours. Now Suhasini went to look for job and she got into a reputed school. She was supported by good staff members. This association was meant to be for lifetime.

It was time for another beginning. Rashmi ma'am was her in-charge. She supported and guided her properly. Any difficulty she could turn to her. She could share any idea with her. With her cooperation she completed 1 year. Asha was another friend in school and a neighbour who encouraged her thoroughly. She was like an anchor. But permanence was not happening soon. Something else was in store for her. Suhasini now knew she had to make a place for herself in the world. She knew life was full of struggles but believed that we have to keep going.

Chapter 8

Suhasini's settlement

Suhasini now wanted to settle down and marry. Everybody had hopes that probably she would have an affair. But where was the time? So, it had to be an arranged marriage through a newspaper advertisement. So, Adarsh Mama, Anita Mami started looking for a suitable boy. In August 2005, they received a bio-data which seemed reasonable. Everyone went ahead and roka was fixed. After the roka, the boy's parents asked if the children could meet.

After few days Suhasini and Vikram started seeing each other. For few days distance was maintained then they started holding hands. Vikram and Suhasini chatted at night. They talked for hours and hours together. Finally on 25th October 2005, Suhasini got married to Vikram Malhotra. They went for their honeymoon to Manali.

Once Suhasini was back, differences started surfacing between them. Suhasini was meanwhile put on probation basis in a school. She was thrilled to hear this piece of news. Finally, her struggle paid off. Vikram never supported her. Suhasini was broken. Finally, they filed for divorce and parted ways after mutual consent. She now decided to put all her energy into work, probably she was not destined to be happily married like other girls.

Chapter 9

A journey of self discovery

After her divorce, Suhasini decided to apply for a job in different schools to start afresh. Luckily, she got into her previous school.

She was happy to be back with her old colleagues. They accepted her gracefully. After working for a year, they put her on probation basis. Life was giving her a second chance. But old demons of memories always hounded her.

Now, Suhasini was talking differently. She was not able to connect with the world. For her Ram was still alive and supporting her. She would only respond on colours and signages on road. She felt somebody was helping her to achieve major goals. Her thoughts had taken over her. Suhasini felt her thoughts could be read by people. Even though it was not true but circumstances led her to believe this. She wouldn't talk. Suhasini was only thinking. Her fears had given her to believe these thoughts. From a fearful person she became a very important person in her own eyes. In this state of mind, it was very difficult to say who is dead and who is living. Even in this difficult time her Principal and close friends supported her.

Doctors had completely lost hope that she could ever recover. She had to be taken care of. So, constant help was required. A 24-hour attendant was hired to take care of Suhasini. The attendant used to go everywhere Suhasini went. Suhasini sometimes used to get irritated with too much of surveillance. But this help was required otherwise she could harm herself or lose herself in a crowd. Suhasini had to be protected. Manjiri was quiet and silently supporting her daughter.

She knew this was a difficult period, but in her heart, she knew 'This too shall pass'. In the meantime, Manjiri sent her to different fairs, bazaars so that she could have an outlet. Manjiri knew it was taking a toll on her financial condition but remembered Jhaijee's words 'you have to sail through bad times with courage and they don't last forever.'

Meanwhile, Manjiri was very particular about giving medicines to Suhasini. Her Mama, Mami were also worried about her health. They were continuously keeping a track of her development. Only her Anita Mami and attendant went to the doctor. Manjiri was not able to go.

At last, after 10 months, when Suhasini visited the doctor, the doctor asked her — "Do you still feel people can read your thoughts?" Suhasini found it funny and refused it. She denied that there were cameras fitted everywhere. At that time the doctor realised that now the medicines are working. There is a sign of improvement. The doctor was happy for Suhasini. Suhasini smiled and felt something had changed around her. She could now connect with people and was talking to people. Manjiri was still apprehensive and felt Suhasini was vulnerable as a baby. After 10 days the attendant was asked to leave.

Suhasini was again back to school but without the attendant. She still had to take medication. The medicines were for lifetime.

Now Suhasini lived happily ever after and was seen taking up new challenges.

About schizophrenia

Schizophrenia is a curable disease. It can be treated with medicines. Medicines are for lifetime. Schizophrenia can happen to anyone anywhere. It is difficult position of mind where outwardly everything seems okay but mentally one is controlled by invalid thoughts. Everyone may try to reason out, but the thoughts are so powerful that one doesn't want to listen to anyone. One's thoughts are so powerful that everything seems minute. It is difficult to monitor thousands of thoughts in a day. But it is negative thoughts i.e., thoughts leading to anxiety, stress and panic can give rise to complications.

Always ask yourself 'Am I being too negative or am I being too anxious?' Write down your thoughts. It will help to pour out. If things do not resolve then see a counsellor or a doctor. Immediate intervention is necessary. Nobody will term you as mad if you seek help. If a thought persists in mind and one is not able to sleep, one should consult a doctor.

There is lot of stigmas attached with mental health. It should be treated at par with physical ailment. One should not ignore the signs or symptoms. Good health should be seen in totality, mental as well as physical. One should remember it's ok to seek help. We are human beings and live in society. In society, it becomes imperative to help each other. That's how the human race will prosper.

Like Suhasini, we all face challenges in life. But the core quality should not change. Suhasini remained honest, upright and clear in her dealings. She never cheated anyone. The whole purpose of her life was to keep looking for best solutions and not become part of the problem. Suhasini retained a child-like quality of being curious and exploring the options for solutions. As they always say after every dark night there is a dawn of new day. Everything that goes up has to come down and vice-versa. There is always a change, it is up to oneself to see positive or negative side. Suhasini was a positive person. One has to remember, the equation of relationship changes with somebody entering your life or somebody exiting it. Even after going through so much, she had the ability to rise to her feet. One must have faith in oneself, faith in the creator. He created you not to go through suffering, but to learn, grow and move ahead in life. The idea is live life QUEENSIZE.

Ingram Content Group UK Ltd.
Milton Keynes UK
UKHW011817140423
420194UK00002B/231